Xmas 1982

The Berenstain Bears' CHRISTMAS TREE

The Berenstain Bears' CHRISTMAS TREE

Stan and Jan Berenstain

Random House 🏠 New York

Library of Congress Cataloging in Publication Data: Berenstain, Stanley. The Berenstain Bears' Christmas tree. SUMMARY: During the Bears' search for a Christmas tree they are reminded of what Christmas is really about. [1. Christmas stories. 2. Bears—Fiction. 3. Stories in rhyme] I. Berenstain, Janice, joint author. II. Title. PZ8.3.B4493Bh [E] 80-5087 ISBN 0-394-84566-8 (trade); 0-394-94566-2 (lib. bdg.)
Manufactured in the United States of America 4 5 6 7 8 9 0

In Bear Country,
Christmas excitement was mounting.
The waiting was down
To ten hours and counting.

The holly was hung.
The presents were bought.
A magnificent Christmas
Salmon was caught.

And now it was time
For the most fun of all—
Getting the tree!

A tree full and fat,
Straight, green, and tall,
With oodles of needles
And crannies and nooks
For the bears to hang
Their tree things by hooks.

"The tree things!" cried Pop
With the jolliest shout.
"Our wonderful tree things!
Let's get them out!"

They had quite a collection.
There were bangles and bells
And bright colored balls—

Boxes of things
In closets and cupboards
And corners of halls!

There were some that were bearlooms
Saved year after year . . .

A Santa Bear sled
With tiny reindeer . . .

Strings of bright beads
To hang in festoons . . .

A musical bear
That sang Christmasy tunes.

TIS THE SEASON
TO BE FURRY
ES-PEC-IALLY
IF YOU'RE A BEAR

But the bears' finest tree thing,
Their finest by far,
Was the thing for the top—
Their Christmas tree star!

It had eighteen points
And was so glittery bright
That the stars of the heavens
Seemed dim in its light.

"What an array!
What a display!"
Papa Bear bragged,
Quite carried away.

"What a grand and glorious
Sight it will be
When we hang all this stuff
On our Christmas tree.

Why, bears will come
From near and far
To see how
Christmasy we are!"

So, all the bears needed now,
Don't you see,
All that they needed now—
Was the tree!

"A tree straight and tall,
Fine, full, and fat.
Come, cubs!" said Papa,
As he put on his hat.

"Now be sure to dress warmly,"
Said wise Mama Bear.
"There's more than a hint
Of snow in the air.

And, oh yes,
Buy our tree down the road
From Grizzly Gus.
I am sure he will have
The right tree for us."

"Snow?" said Papa,
Sniffing the air.
"Not a chance!
The weather today
Will be bright and fair.
I always can tell
If it's going to snow
By a sharp shooting pain
In my left big toe!"

"As for Gus and those trees
Lying in stacks—
Not for us!" Papa said,
As he took up his ax.
"But, Papa," said Brother,
"I don't mean to fuss,
But Mom said to *buy* one
From Grizzly Gus!"
"One of *those?*" snorted Pa.
"Fresh cut, indeed!
They look more like some
Overgrown evergreen weed!"

Now, Brother and Sister
Usually did what Mom said.
But not Papa—
He did whatever
Came into his head.

And a fine fat tree
Is what came into his head
That particular Christmas.

"No matter what! No matter where!
If it means going down to the Panama Isthmus!
If it means climbing up to the top of Pikes Peak!
I will find it," he said, "if it takes us a week!"

"But Christmas," said Sis, "is just hours away!
We must find our Christmas tree, today!"

But Pop didn't hear.
By now, he was really quite carried away.

He was forgetting something that day—
That Christmas is more than show and display.
More than just tinsel and pink plastic stars,
And stuffing yourself with sugar-nut bars.

There was something IMPORTANT
That he was forgetting—
Christmas is for *giving!*
It isn't for *getting*.

This was a time to be thinking of others—
Mamas, papas, sisters, brothers,
A time to think of each neighbor and friend.
But, all *that* was forgotten
As they rounded a bend.

As they rounded that bend,
What did they see?

PAPA'S PERFECT CHRISTMAS TREE!

What a tree! What a tree!
This surely was it!
Its green was so green!
Its tall didn't quit!
Its nooks all had crannies.
Its crannies had nooks.
The one question was—
Would they have enough hooks?

"Stand back!" said Papa,
Getting ready to chop.

"Wait!" Sister cried.
"Hold it, please. STOP!"

On the timely advice
Of small Sister Bear,
Pa managed to stop
His ax in midair!

And a good thing, too—
For that Christmas tree's trunk

Just happened to be
The home of a skunk!

And some squirrels and a grouse,
And one small chipmunk
Also resided in that
Christmas tree's trunk.

Plus twenty-six crows,
Who were renting upstairs.
And not one of them happy
To see those three bears!

"Though this tree," said Pa,
"Seemed a find,
It isn't quite . . ."

"WHAT I HAD IN MIND!"

There was something else
Pa hadn't in mind
As they rapidly left
Mr. Skunk's tree behind.

The coming great day
Was the skunk's Christmas, too.
And the squirrels',
And the chipmunk's.
If he chopped down their tree,
What would they do?

And the crows and the grouse,
What would *they* do
If he chopped down their house?

Where would they have *their* holly and bells?
Their Christmas goodies? *Their* Christmasy smells?
How would they enjoy *their* Christmas feast?
But such questions as those did not bother Papa,
Not in the least.

His head was so filled with *his* bangles and bells,
His bright colored balls,
His tree things stacked up in closets and halls,
That there just wasn't *room* for anything more.

"Onward!" he cried.
And the bears pressed on
With their Christmas tree chore.

"We will find the right tree.
We must and we will!

I will ford any stream!

Climb any hill!

Go over Niagara Falls
on a log!"

"Penetrate
The impenetrable fog!

Brave the terrors
Of Sinister Bog!

We will find
The Christmas tree we seek.
We will find it," said he,
"If it takes us a week!"

"But, please!" said Sister.
"We must find a tree soon!"

"She's right, Dad," said Brother.
"It's late afternoon!"

"A tree," cried Papa,
"Fine, full, and fat,
Straight, green, and tall . . ."

And at that very moment,
The snow Mom predicted
Started to fall.

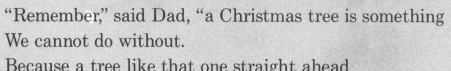

"Remember," said Dad, "a Christmas tree is something
We cannot do without.
Because a tree like that one straight ahead
IS WHAT CHRISTMAS IS *ABOUT!*"

Then, without so much
As a passing thought
About whether he should
Or whether he ought,
He raised his ax
And got ready to chop.
"STAND BACK!" he said,
Reckoning where
The tree would drop.

It was quite a fine tree—
Sedate and tall,
Graceful and regal.
It was also, it happened—

The home of an eagle!

And a hawk!

And a wolf!

And a great snowy owl!

The eagle took off,
While the hawk
And the wolf
And the great snowy owl
Set up a terrible,
terrible howl!

The noise seemed to come
From every direction.
Then . . .

Mr. Eagle
Expressed *his* objection!

"No, that tree back there
Wasn't quite it.
Its green was too green,
And it leaned a bit.

It wasn't quite
What I had in mind.
Come! We still have
A tree to find!"

Completely ignoring Papa's big toe,
The snow had become a really big snow!
A snow of snows! A blizzard of blizzards!
Why, there was snow on the ground
Up to their gizzards!
"Up the mountain! Follow me!
I'll find one soon!
You'll see! You'll see!"

"I certainly hope so,"
Said Sister, quite worried.

"That's right," added Brother.
"In a snow like this,
A bear could get buried!"

But, Papa pressed on
With just one thing in mind—
That perfect tree
He was going to find.
"Full and fat," he cried.
"Tall and green,
The finest tree
You've ever seen."

"Now, THAT is the kind
Of tree I mean!"

"Hurry!" said Sister.
"Chop it down!"
"Yes!" said Brother.
"We still have time
To get back to town!"

But Pop was silent as he looked at that tree.
Strangely silent. What did he see?

What Papa saw
Through the driving snow
Was a *tiny window!*
Within: a glow.

Pop hardly breathed!
He spoke not a word!
What he saw through the window
Was a tiny snowbird
Busily trimming *his*
Christmas tree
With the help of the members
Of *his* family.

Their tree was a twig
Decorated with seeds,
That the tiny snowbirds
Had collected from weeds.

And for the first time
That day . . .

Papa saw Christmas
In a different way.

Maybe it was
The tiny twig tree,
Or maybe the seeds
That helped Papa see
The other guy's needs.

But whatever it was, Pa shouldered his ax
And spared the tree.
He remembered what Christmas is really about.
He'd had it all backward and inside out.

"This," said Pop,
With a far-off Christmasy
Look in his eye,
"Is a time to think
Of the other guy.
A time," he continued,
"To be thinking of others—
Mamas, papas,
Sisters, brothers.
Nature's creatures,
Great and small,
Fellow creatures,
One and all."

"But, Papa!" said Sis.
"What about *our* tree?
The tree for our bells?
Our bright colored balls?"

"Yeah!" added Brother.
"And all that stuff
In our closets and halls?"

"No problem," said Pa.
"There's no need to fuss.
We'll go back and buy one
From Grizzly Gus."

"GRIZZLY GUS?"
Both cubs said together.
"After that trip?
And that climb?
And this weather?"

"Don't bother me
With questions," said Pop.
Then he found an old stump
And started to chop.
And quick as a flash
There were three pairs of skis.
"Here," Papa said,
"Slip into these."

So, Pop and the cubs
Put on skis
And went back for one
Of Old Grizzly's trees.

But when they got back
To the Christmas tree lot,
The *lot* was still there,

But the trees were not!

Only a sign
Saying, SORRY, SOLD OUT,
And some tired old needles
Lying about.

When Sis saw those needles—
Well, she thought she might cry.
But then something *wondrous*
Caught her eye!

"LOOK!" she shouted—

"Somebody has decorated our HOUSE!"

And somebody had—
The chipmunk, the skunk,
The crows, and the grouse,
The eagle, the owl,
And all of the others,
And quite a few
Of their sisters and brothers,
Were returning the kindness
Pa showed those snowbirds.

The bears, they were speechless.
They just had no words.

All of the bears'
Tree things were there—
The bangles, the bells,
The musical bear,
The Christmas tree star,
The Santa Bear sled. . . .

"Why, everything's shining!"
Sister suddenly said.

Then a very special starry light
Filled the sky that Christmas Eve night.
It didn't come from that pink plastic star.
It was the light of the *real* Christmas Star!

The true Christmas spirit shone down that night.
It filled the whole sky with a lovely light.
It charged the cold, clear Bear Country air.
It filled the heart of every bear,

And their fellow creatures,
One and all,
Nature's creatures,
Great and small.

Next day, at dinner, Brother Bear wondered,
"Pop, on that thinking-of-others bit—
How about the salmon?
How about *it*?"

"Your remark," said Papa,
"Shows wit and perception.
But in the case of the salmon,
We'll make an exception!"